THE DAY I BECAME A BIRD

To Guridi. Thank you for the beautiful
moments we've shared over our books. — I.C.

Thank you, Candela — G.

THE DAY I BECAME A BIRD

INGRID CHABBERT
GURIDI

Kids Can Press

The day I started school, I fell in love.

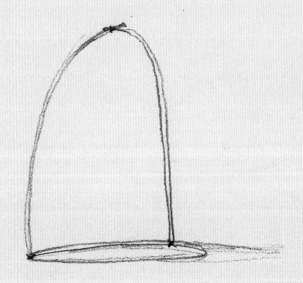

It was the first time.

At home that night, I drew a picture of her.
Then another. And another.

And one with hearts and a smiling sun.

Sylvia is in my class.
She sits in front of me.
All I see is her.
But she doesn't see me.

DIAGRAMS OF PARTS OF A BIRD

Sylvia is a bird lover.
She can't bear to see them living in cages.
She quietly observes them in the wild and
gently cares for them when they are injured.

There are birds on her pants and dresses.
She wears bird barrettes in her hair.
She draws birds on her notebooks and folders.
And when she speaks, her voice sounds like birdsong.

Sylvia only has eyes for birds.

When I look at her, I forget about everything else.

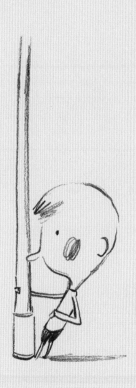

CETTI'S
WARBLER

EUROPEAN
GOLDEN PLOVER

My toy cars, soccer and all the rest
don't seem important.
    And I don't look at birds the same way
I did before.

So one morning, I decide to dress up as a bird.

A large bird, with shining feathers.

Like the ones you see in the forest in summer.

I feel handsome in this costume. (And very warm.)

I dream that, one day, I'll land somewhere in the Rocky Mountains or at the top of a pyramid.

With Sylvia, maybe ...

Everyone stares at me at school.

Some kids giggle, too, but I don't care.

I don't want to take off my costume — I am a bird.

But it isn't easy to walk around in this thing!
Going to the bathroom is even more complicated.

And it's hard to keep my balance when I play soccer.

Climbing trees is much harder, too.

The worst is when it rains. I smell like wet dog!

Then one afternoon, I come
face to face with Sylvia.

And finally our eyes meet.

Sylvia steps closer to me and takes off my costume.
I don't know what to do.
My heart is beating a hundred miles an hour.
In the sky, I see a flock of birds take flight.
Sylvia puts her arms around me.
I stand perfectly still. I can't think.

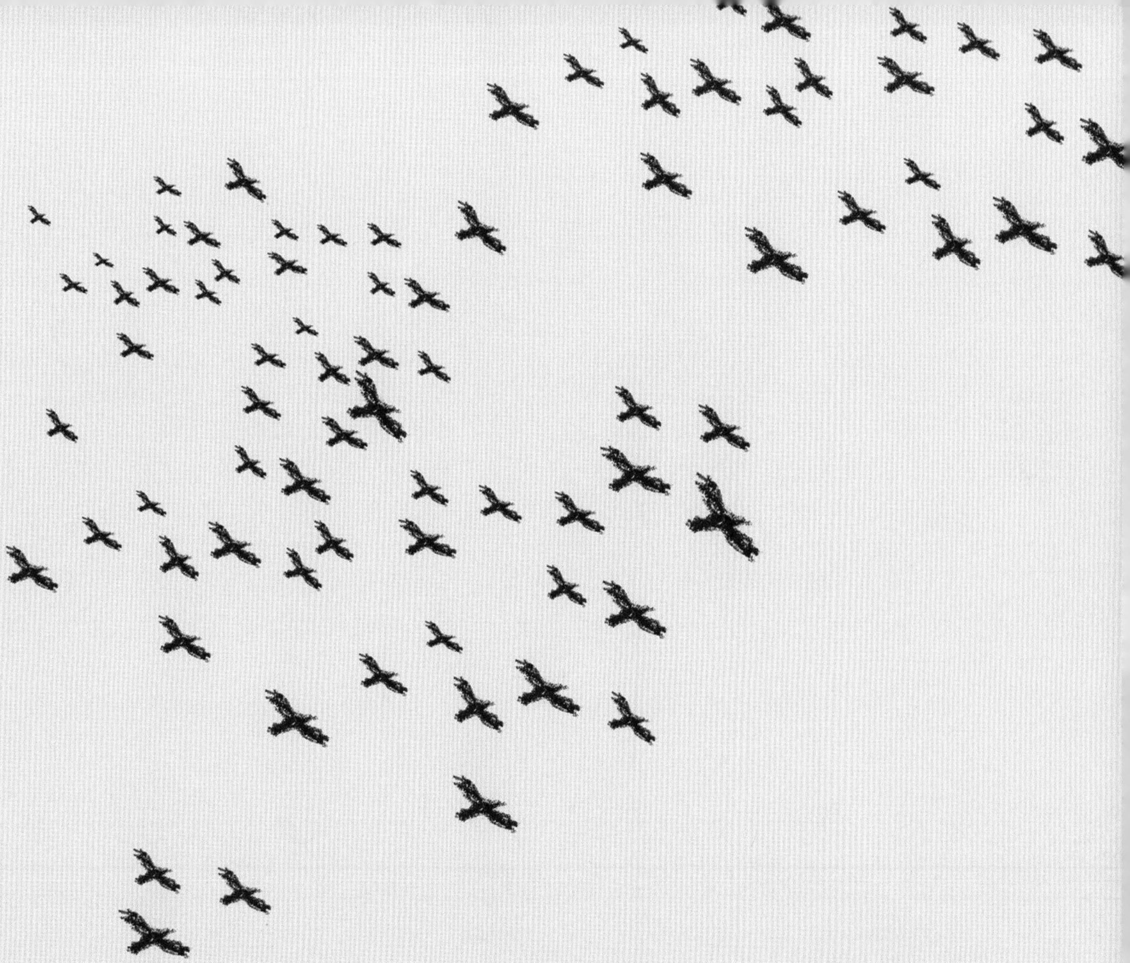

I'm not a bird anymore, but I feel like I'm flying.

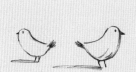

This edition published by Kids Can Press in 2016

Originally published in Spain under the title *El dia en que me converti en un pájaro*
by Ediciones TTT, S.C.

Kids Can Press acknowledges the financial support of the Government of Ontario,
through the Ontario Media Development Corporation's Ontario Book Initiative.

Published in Canada by
Kids Can Press Ltd.
25 Dockside Drive
Toronto, ON M5A 0B5

Published in the U.S. by
Kids Can Press Ltd.
2250 Military Road
Tonawanda, NY 14150

www.kidscanpress.com

The artwork in this book was rendered in pencil and photoshop.
The text is set in Cloister.

English edition edited by Yvette Ghione

This edition is smyth sewn casebound.
Manufactured in Malaysia, in 3/2016 by Tien Wah Press (Pte.) Ltd.

CM 16 0 9 8 7 6 5 4 3 2 1

Library and Archives Canada Cataloguing in Publication

Chabbert, Ingrid, 1978–

[Dia en que me converti en un pájaro. English]

The day I became a bird / written by Ingrid Chabbert ; illustrated by Raúl Nieto Guridi.

Translation of: El dia en que me converti en un pájaro.

ISBN 978-1-77138-621-0 (bound)

I. Nieto Guridi, Raúl, 1970–, illustrator II. Title. III. Title: Dia en que me
converti en un pájaro. English

PZ7.C349D39 2016   j863'.7   C2015-907980-2

Kids Can Press is a *Corus*™ Entertainment company